Emma
the Easter
Fairy

Special thanks to Tracey West

ISBN 978-0-545-36833-9

12 11 10 9 8 7 6 5 4 3 2 1   11 12 13 14 15 16/0

Printed in the U.S.A.   40

This edition first printing, March 2011

Emma
the Easter
Fairy

by Daisy Meadows

SCHOLASTIC INC.

New York   Toronto   London   Auckland
Sydney   Mexico City   New Delhi   Hong Kong

The Easter Bunny's Cottage

Jack Frost's Ice Castle

Mr. Hopper's Market

Daffodil Field

Kirsty's House

The Sweet Treat Disaster

Easter candy tastes so sweet,
Colored eggs are a pretty treat.
And children smile on Easter Day
When the Easter Bunny comes their way.

But I'll make chocolate melt away.
There won't be colored eggs today.
And nobody will think it's funny,
When I kidnap the Easter Bunny!

**Find the hidden letters in the chicks
throughout this book. Unscramble all 9 letters
to spell a special Easter word!**

Contents

A Melted Mess!

"We're finally here!" Rachel Walker cried as her dad pulled the car to a stop in the driveway.

Rachel's best friend, Kirsty Tate, ran across the lawn to greet her.

"We've got so many fun things planned," Kirsty said as Rachel got out of the car. "We're going to dye eggs

for the big Easter
egg hunt, and go to
Strawberry Farm,
and—"

"First we have
to unpack," Mrs.
Walker said with
a smile. "Rachel, why don't you and
Kirsty grab the cooler?"

Rachel and Kirsty each took a handle
of the blue cooler and carried it toward
Kirsty's house.

"I'm so glad your Aunt Sally lives near
Wetherbury," Kirsty said.

"Me, too," agreed Rachel. "We'll
have Easter dinner with Aunt Sally, but
first we get to spend two whole days
with you!" The two girls had met on
vacation at Rainspell Island. They were

always excited to have a chance to visit each other.

They carried the cooler up the steps to Kirsty's front door.

"This is heavy!" Kirsty remarked. "What's in it?"

Rachel grinned. "It's a special surprise."

When they entered the kitchen, Rachel's parents were talking with Mr. and Mrs. Tate.

"Good to see you, Rachel," said Kirsty's mom. "What are you carrying in that big cooler?"

"Can I tell them, Mom?" Rachel asked.

Mrs. Walker nodded, smiling.

"Mom and I made special Easter chocolates," Rachel said. "There are bunnies, flowers, chicks, and even chocolate eggs. We wrapped them in sparkly paper, too! They look so pretty."

Rachel opened the lid to show them. "Oh, no!" She gasped.

"What's wrong?" Kirsty asked. Inside the cooler, the chocolates had melted into one big, gooey mess! The sparkly wrappers had

slipped off and fallen into the sticky chocolate.

"They're all ruined!" Rachel cried.

Mrs. Walker looked over Rachel's shoulder and frowned. "That's odd," she said. She felt the inside of the lid. "We filled that cooler with plenty of ice packs. It still feels chilly inside. The chocolates shouldn't have melted."

Rachel tried not to look too sad, but

she couldn't help it. "But they did. Now there's no chocolate for Easter."

"Don't forget about the Easter Bunny," Mrs. Tate reminded her. "I'm sure he'll bring you lots of chocolate in your Easter basket."

"He always does," Kirsty said, trying to cheer up her friend.

"I'd better clean this up," said Rachel's mom. "Why don't you girls go outside for a while? It's a beautiful day."

The girls headed outside and sat on Kirsty's front porch. Pretty pink and yellow tulips bloomed in the flowerbed there.

"It's strange that the candy melted, even though the cooler was chilly," Kirsty remarked.

Rachel nodded. "I was thinking the

same thing," she said. She lowered her voice. "Do you think Jack Frost is behind it somehow?"

The girls had a special secret. They were friends with the fairies! Because of that, they knew Jack Frost and his goblins were always causing trouble in Fairyland. Sometimes they played their tricks in the human world, too.

"Maybe," Kirsty replied. "But it's hard to believe there could be goblins around on a nice sunny day like today."

"A beautiful day won't keep the goblins away!" a musical voice cried just then.

One of the pink tulips began to wiggle. The petals opened up, and a tiny fairy flew out! The air shimmered around her as she flew toward the girls.

"You must be Rachel and Kirsty," said the fairy, twirling in the air. "I'm Emma the Easter Fairy!"

Emma wore a pastel yellow dress with a pretty pink sash around the waist. She had polka-dotted rain boots on her feet, and her bouncy

curls were held back with a flowery headband.

"It's nice to meet you," Rachel said.

"Hi, Emma," said Kirsty. "Happy Easter!"

"I'm afraid there might not be a happy Easter this year," Emma said, perching on Kirsty's shoulder and looking glum. "The Easter Bunny is missing!"

Emma's Story

"Missing!" Rachel exclaimed. "Did Jack Frost kidnap him?"

"I'll bet he did," Kirsty said. "Jack Frost has done things like that before. Remember the time he stole Santa's sleigh?"

"That's exactly what I thought," Emma said. "But he's getting even trickier! Let me show you."

Emma waved her wand, and in a burst of sparkles, two Easter eggs appeared in midair. Rachel and Kirsty each took one. Each eggshell was painted with pretty flowers.

"Look through the pointy end," Emma told them.

Each of the eggs had a small window on one end. Both girls looked through the windows.

"It's Fairyland!" Rachel exclaimed.

"That's right," Emma said. "And that's my cottage."

Thanks to Emma's fairy magic, they could see inside Emma's red-and-white toadstool cottage. Emma was happily painting Easter eggs with a paintbrush. A white chicken perched on the chair behind her, watching.

"It's my job to add the extra sparkle to Easter," Emma explained. "Every year, my pet chicken, Fluffy, lays three magical eggs. On the first egg, I paint a picture of a chocolate bunny. That egg helps to make Easter candy extra yummy."

"Mmm," said Kirsty, licking her lips. "I love Easter candy."

"On the second egg, I paint a picture of a colorful Easter egg," Emma told them. "That egg helps make all of the  dyed Easter eggs bright and beautiful."

"So that's why Easter eggs always look so pretty!" Rachel said.

Emma nodded, looking proud. "On the third egg, I paint an Easter basket," the fairy went on. "That's the most important egg of all! It gives the Easter Bunny the extra magical push he needs to deliver millions of Easter baskets in just one night."

The girls held their eggs to their eyes again and watched the story unfold. They saw Emma put the finishing touches on her final painted egg. Then she smiled, gave Fluffy a pat on the head, and flew off.

"I wanted to tell the Easter Bunny that I had finished the eggs," Emma said. "But when I got to his cottage, he wasn't there! I looked all over Fairyland, but I couldn't find him."

In the pictures, the girls saw Emma flying around Fairyland. Finally she went to the castle to find Queen Titania and King Oberon.

"I told them that the Easter Bunny was missing," Emma explained. "Right away, they suspected Jack Frost. Last year, he tried to use a spell to turn all of

the Easter eggs rotten. The Easter Bunny
stopped him, and Jack Frost has been
angry ever since."

"That proves it!" Kirsty said, looking
defiant. "Jack Frost *must* have kidnapped
the Easter Bunny!"

"Watch and see," Emma said.

In the pictures, Emma followed the
king and queen as they rushed to Jack

Frost's Ice Castle. Jack
Frost sat on his icy
throne, grinning.

"He told us he had
no idea where the
Easter Bunny was,"
Emma said. "He
invited the king and
queen to search the castle.
But the Easter Bunny was nowhere to be
found."

"So was Jack Frost telling the truth?"
Rachel asked.

"It looked that way,"
Emma said. "But
then I suddenly
remembered the three
magic eggs in my
cottage. I had a bad

feeling about them, so I flew back home as quickly as I could."

The picture inside the eggs changed again. Emma flew toward her little toadstool cottage. The girls could see Jack Frost's goblins heading toward her house, too! Emma waved her wand, and silver glitter floated through the air.

The magic glitter trickled inside the cottage and surrounded the three magic eggs. The eggs disappeared just as the

goblins burst through the
door. They were safe!

"I sent the eggs here to
Wetherbury," Emma said.
"I don't know where they
ended up, but they should
be safe from the goblins."

"But not for long," Rachel pointed out.
"We need to find them first."

"Not only that," Kirsty added, "but
we have to find the Easter Bunny, too!"

Goblins in the Market

"Emma, is that why our Easter chocolates melted?" Rachel asked. "Because the magic eggs are missing?"

Emma nodded, and her curls bounced against her shoulders. "Yes. And that's not all. The Easter candy won't taste nice. The Easter eggs will go bad. And worst of all, the Easter Bunny won't be

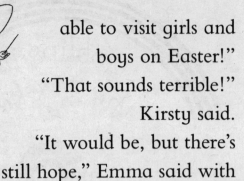

able to visit girls and boys on Easter!"

"That sounds terrible!" Kirsty said.

"It would be, but there's still hope," Emma said with a smile. "Especially now that I have you two girls to help me."

Rachel jumped up. "You said the eggs are somewhere here in Wetherbury. We should start looking right away!"

"Wetherbury is a big place," Kirsty reminded her. "It will be hard to find three small eggs."

Rachel was thoughtful. "Maybe we should start looking in places where you'd normally find eggs."

"Like the market!" Kirsty chimed in.

Just then, the girls heard footsteps

coming toward the front door.

"Emma, hide!" Rachel said in a loud whisper.

Poof! Emma vanished, leaving a trail of fairy dust shimmering in the air behind her.

And just in time! A second later, Mrs. Tate and Mrs. Walker stepped onto the porch.

"How are you girls doing?" Mrs. Tate asked.

"Fine, Mom," Kirsty said. "We were thinking of taking a walk. Do you need anything from the market?"

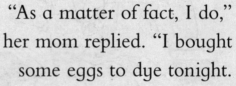

"As a matter of fact, I do," her mom replied. "I bought some eggs to dye tonight. But they seem to have gone bad already. It's very strange! Mr. Hopper always sells nice, fresh eggs."

"Maybe they were a bad batch," Mrs. Walker suggested.

Rachel and Kirsty looked at each other. They knew that Emma's missing magic was the real reason the eggs went bad.

"We'll get some more," Kirsty offered.

Mrs. Tate gave Kirsty money for the eggs, and the girls headed to the village center on foot.

"Wetherbury is very nice," Emma said, suddenly fluttering in the air next to them. "All the pretty flowers remind me of Fairyland."

"Thank you," Kirsty said. "Fairyland is beautiful, too."

"But there still isn't any sign of the Easter Bunny there," Emma said. "I hope we can find him soon!"

As they turned the corner, they walked past the pet shop. The sign on the door read Closed for the Holiday.

Emma suddenly shivered.

"Emma, are you cold?" Rachel asked, concerned.

"No, this is a different kind of shiver," Emma replied. "Fairies can sense when magic is near. It makes us feel tickly all over." She looked around. "I don't see any other fairies here, do you?"

Rachel and Kirsty looked everywhere, but they couldn't see any other fairies. "No," Rachel said. "And that reminds me—you should hide, before someone sees you!" "Oh!" Emma said, fluttering around. She settled inside the pocket of Rachel's pink dress. "Is this all right?" "Just keep your head down," Kirsty whispered. Only she and Rachel knew about the fairies and their magic,

and they had promised
to keep them a secret.
A few minutes later,
they finally arrived
at Mr. Hopper's Market.
They opened the door, and a blast of
cool air hit them.

"*Now* I'm shivering because I'm cold!"
Emma called up from her hiding place.

Right next to the front door was an
Easter display. A big stuffed Easter
Bunny sat on a mound of fake grass.

GET
YOUR
EASTER
GEAR
HERE

← EXIT

He held a basket of colorful plastic eggs. A sign on the display read GET YOUR EASTER GEAR HERE!

A long line of people waited at the cash register. They were all holding bags of candy, and they didn't look very happy. Behind the counter, Mr. Hopper looked awfully worried.

Two boys in baseball caps were arguing over by the candy aisle.

"*I* want the green jellybeans!" one boy yelled.

"No, *I* want the green jellybeans!" shouted the other.

Kirsty spotted her friend Andy waiting in line.

"Andy, why is it so crowded in here?" she asked him.

"Something's wrong with Mr. Hopper's candy," Andy replied. "All the chocolate is melted, even though it's freezing in here. And most of it just doesn't taste right." He held out an open bag of jellybeans. "These taste terrible! You should try one."

Rachel and Kirsty looked at each other. Eating gross jellybeans didn't sound like fun, but they had to see for themselves.

Kirsty carefully picked out a white jellybean from the bag. Rachel

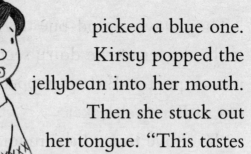

picked a blue one. Kirsty popped the jellybean into her mouth. Then she stuck out her tongue. "This tastes like onions!" she cried.

Rachel made a face. "Mine tastes like blue cheese. *Yuck!*"

"Mom wants me to get my money back," Andy said.

Kirsty sighed. "Poor Mr. Hopper!"

Rachel tapped her on the shoulder. "Kirsty, we should go get those eggs for your mom." She lowered her voice so only Kirsty could hear. "Maybe we'll find a magic egg there, too."

They waved good-bye to Andy and walked over to the dairy section, where it was quieter. Emma popped her head out of Kirsty's pocket.

"We have to find the magic egg that makes Easter candy delicious — and fast!" she said anxiously.

"Let's start looking through these egg cartons," Rachel suggested.

But before they could, some loud shouts came from the candy aisle. The two fighting boys were now wrestling over the bag of green jellybeans. They rolled right by the girls.

"Give it to me!" one boy cried.

"Never!" replied the other.

The girls jumped back to get out of their way. Then Rachel noticed

something. Both boys wore baseball caps and jeans. But they didn't have any shoes on their feet . . . their *green* feet.

"Kirsty, those aren't boys at all!" she whispered. "They're goblins!"

The Jellybean Trail

The girls hurried to the cereal aisle, where the goblins couldn't see them.

"I should have known!" Kirsty said. "Only goblins would fight over green jellybeans."

"They're here for the same reason we are," Emma piped up. "To find the missing magic eggs!"

"Then we have to find them first," Rachel said.

Kirsty nodded. "And we have to get those goblins out of here before someone sees them."

The girls heard more shouting from the dairy aisle. They peeked around a shelf and saw three more goblins in disguise, opening up all of the egg cartons! Eggs spilled and cracked on the floor as the goblins carelessly pawed through them.

"Oh, no! What if one of the magic eggs is in there?" Kirsty asked.

Rachel looked thoughtful. She had an idea! "We know that goblins like green jellybeans. Emma, can you use your magic to make some?"

Emma flew out of Rachel's pocket. "Of course! I'm the Easter Fairy. Jellybeans are my specialty!"

"Perfect," Rachel said. "If you make a long trail of green jellybeans from the goblins to the front door, the goblins will follow them outside."

"That's a great idea!" Kirsty agreed. "Just make sure no one sees you, Emma."

37

Luckily, the customers in the store were too upset about their melted chocolate to notice the goblins. Careful to stay out of sight, Emma flew into the dairy aisle and waved her wand. Green sparkles shot from it. When the sparkles hit the floor, they turned into green jellybeans!

Emma made a trail of green jellybeans all the way down the aisle. It didn't take long for the goblins to notice.

"Look — green jellybeans!" one of them cried out.

The two wrestling goblins stopped fighting immediately. The other goblins

dropped their egg cartons. All five
of them started to race after the
jellybeans.

"It's working!" Kirsty cheered quietly.

Emma made a magical trail of
jellybeans that led all the way to the
front door. The goblins followed the
trail, scooping up the jellybeans as they
appeared. They shoved and pushed each
other to get to them.

Rachel and Kirsty watched the goblins
from a distance. Once the goblins were
outside, the girls would be able to safely
look for the missing magic eggs.

But the goblins stopped before they
went through the front door of the
market.

"What's happening?" Rachel
wondered.

One of the goblins had spotted Mr.
Hopper's Easter display. "I think I see
something," he said, squinting.

The goblin stuck his hand inside the
basket of plastic eggs. Then he pulled
out an egg that was glimmering with
fairy magic. The egg was white, with a
picture of a chocolate bunny painted
on it.

"I've found one of the missing eggs!" the goblin howled. "Wait until Jack Frost sees this!"

With that, the goblins cheered and raced through the door.

Rachel and Kirsty dashed to catch up to them. "We can't let them get away!" Kirsty cried.

Help From the Sky

The girls found Emma hovering outside
the market door.

"Oh, dear!" she said. "My jellybean
trail led those goblins right to the magic
egg. What bad luck!"

"They're headed for the park," Kirsty
said, pointing. "We can catch up if we
hurry."

The girls ran fast and nearly caught up to the goblins. But the goblins kept going! They ran right into the woods at the edge of the park.

"We could lose them in the trees," Rachel worried.

"But we won't," Emma said. "Hold still!"

Emma waved her wand and fairy dust sprinkled out and swirled around the girls. The whirling cloud of glittering

dust swept them off of their feet. The
girls could feel themselves
getting smaller, but
they weren't afraid.
This had happened
to them before.

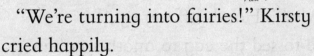

"We're turning into fairies!" Kirsty
cried happily.

"Now we can all fly around the trees
and catch up to the goblins," Emma told
them.

Rachel took off. "Let's go!"

Rachel was the first to reach the goblin carrying the magic egg. She swooped down and tried to grab it, but the goblin spotted her.

"Hey, it's a fairy!" The goblin scowled. "Hands off my egg!"

He tossed the egg to another goblin.

Kirsty flew as fast as she could, hoping to scoop the egg out of the air. But the other goblin jumped up and grabbed it.

"Ha, ha! You can't get it!" the goblin taunted, holding up the egg.

Emma flew down and tried to take the egg from him. But one of his friends warned him. "Behind you!"

The goblin turned and saw Emma just in time. He threw the egg to another one of his friends.

"This is a fun game!" the goblin said with a nasty smile. "Keep away from the fairies!"

Kirsty flew up to Rachel. "They're too fast!"

At that moment, Emma began to sing a song. It didn't have any words. But it sounded pretty, almost like a bird singing.

Rachel and Kirsty looked at each other. Why was Emma singing at a time like this?

Caw! Caw! Caw!

Five beautiful blue jays swooped down from the trees, drawn by Emma's song. She had called them to help!

"Friends, please help us get the magic egg back from these goblins!" Emma called out.

The birds dove at the goblin holding the egg. They pecked at his head with their black beaks. Startled, the goblin

dropped the magic egg. One of the blue
jays broke free and grabbed the egg in
its claws before it reached the ground.

"Get those birds!" the goblin cried.

But the blue jays dove at the other
goblins. The goblins were so scared that
they forgot all about the magic egg!
Instead, they shrieked and ran away.

Giggling, Emma sprinkled fairy dust
on Rachel and Kirsty again, and they

turned back into girls. One of the blue
jays flew up and gently dropped the egg
in Rachel's palm.

"Thank you so much, my
friends!" Emma told
the blue jays.

The birds flew in a
circle around the girls
and Emma, tweeting
happily. Then they
sailed off into the trees.

"We did it!" the girls cheered.

"Yes, we did," Emma said happily.
"And now I've got to get this magic egg
back to Fairyland. I'll give it to the king
and queen so they can keep it safe."

Emma waved her wand and sprinkled
fairy dust over the egg, shrinking it back

to fairy-size. Then Emma took the egg from Rachel.

"Good-bye, girls—thanks for your help!" Emma said, blowing them each a kiss. "I'll see you soon!" Then she vanished.

"At least one magic egg is safe," Rachel said.

"That's good," agreed Kirsty. "But now, we'd better get back to Mr. Hopper's and buy those eggs for my mom."

Back at the market, the girls found one carton of eggs that the goblins hadn't broken. They also found a crowd of happy—but confused!—customers.

"Hey, my chocolate bunny isn't melted anymore," said one man.

Another woman chomped on some jellybeans. "And these are delicious!"

"It looks like the Easter candy is yummy again," Kirsty remarked.

Rachel grinned. "Maybe we should try some, just to be sure."

That night, the girls nibbled on chocolate chicks while they dyed Easter eggs. Mrs. Tate gave them six small cups. The girls put a pellet of dye in each cup and added some vinegar. Soon different bubbling bright colors filled the cups: pink, yellow, green, purple, blue, and orange.

"It's almost like fairy magic," Kirsty

whispered as she dipped an egg into the yellow dye.

"I hope they turn out bright and beautiful," Rachel worried. "The magic egg that gives Easter eggs their extra sparkle is still missing."

"And so is the egg that helps the Easter Bunny," Kirsty added.

Kirsty gently put her yellow egg on

a paper towel to dry. As she did, the shell started to crack and break. The egg started to wiggle. Then Emma popped out of the egg and flew up with a giggle!

"I'm sorry I broke your egg," she said. "It's just such a fun way to get into your world."

"That's okay, we have a lot," Kirsty said. "We're dyeing them for the big Easter egg hunt tomorrow at Daffodil Field. Wetherbury holds one every year on the day before Easter."

"That sounds like fun," Emma said. She scratched her head and looked nervous. "But we're so close to Easter, and we still haven't found the Easter Bunny!"

"We still have a whole day to find him," Rachel assured her.

"Yes, and you still have *us* to help you," Kirsty reminded her.

Emma brightened. "You're right! If anyone can find the Easter Bunny, we can!"

Rotten Egg Hunt

Contents

A Magical Feeling

"Are you sure it's okay if we head out early?" Kirsty's mom asked as she put on her coat. "We volunteered to help hide the eggs for the big Easter egg hunt, so we need to beat the crowd."

It was the morning before Easter. Rachel and Kirsty had stayed up past their bedtime, whispering about all the adventures they'd had the day before. Now they were finishing the delicious blueberry pancakes Mrs. Tate had made for breakfast.

"It's fine, Mom," Kirsty said, smiling. "We'll meet you at Daffodil Field when the Easter egg hunt starts."

That will give us some time to figure out how we're going to find the rest of the missing eggs, Kirsty thought. *And the Easter Bunny, too!*

Outside, a car horn beeped. Mrs. Tate gave each of the girls a quick kiss. "See you later! I bet you'll both find lots of eggs," she said before hurrying out the door.

Rachel yawned. "How many eggs do they hide for the egg hunt?" she asked Kirsty.

"There must be hundreds!" Kirsty replied, her eyes shining brightly with excitement. "The entire field is covered with blooming daffodils. The eggs are hidden all over the field."

"That sounds pretty," Rachel said dreamily.

Just then, the air over the table shimmered for a moment.

"I love daffodils!" a voice called out cheerfully. Emma appeared in the air, flapping her wings and grinning. "They're always in bloom at Easter."

Rachel waved hello to her fairy friend. "You should come to the egg hunt," she suggested.

Kirsty nodded. "You would love it. Besides, an Easter egg hunt would be a perfect hiding place for a magic egg, wouldn't it?"

Emma clapped her hands together. "Oh, you're right!" she cried happily. "Can we go there now?"

Kirsty looked at the clock. "They don't let kids on the field until the eggs are hidden. But even if we leave now, we won't have to wait for long."

"Then let's go!" Emma said eagerly. "Tomorrow is Easter. Time is running out!"

The girls quickly cleaned up their breakfast dishes, changed out of their pajamas, and headed to Daffodil Field. Their walk took them through Wetherbury, past the downtown shops.

Emma started to shiver as they passed the pet shop. "There's that magical feeling again," she said, looking around. Mr. Hopper's store was right down the street. "I wonder what it could be."

"Yesterday we found the magic egg in the market after you shivered," Kirsty

said. "Maybe there's another one there."

"We could check," Rachel suggested.

"Okay, but be on the lookout for Jack Frost's goblins," Emma warned. Then she darted out of sight into Kirsty's sweater pocket.

Things were much cleaner and quieter in the market that morning. There were no long lines of people making complaints. The jellybeans and broken

eggs had all been cleaned up. But behind
the counter, Mr. Hopper looked sad.

"Is everything okay, Mr. Hopper?"
Kirsty asked.

Mr. Hopper had
gray hair and a
round face. He
pushed his
eyeglasses up on his
nose when he saw Kirsty.

"Oh, it's nothing, dear. Tomorrow is Easter, after all, and that's a happy day," he said, trying to smile. "And my chocolate has stopped melting. But today, I found that all of the eggs in the refrigerator were rotten! I had to throw them away."

Rachel and Kirsty glanced at one another. They knew why the eggs were rotten!

Mr. Hopper pointed to the refrigerator case, which was empty. "It's terrible not to have any eggs for Easter," he went on. "But I have a new shipment coming in this afternoon. I hope *those* eggs are all right."

"I'm sure they will be," Kirsty assured him.

Mr. Hopper patted her on the shoulder. "That's nice of you to say. Is there anything I can get for you?" he asked.

"Not right now," Kirsty replied. There were clearly no more magic eggs at Mr. Hopper's market. There were no eggs at *all*! "We're going to Daffodil Field."

"Have fun, girls," Mr. Hopper said with a smile.

As the girls left the market, Emma flew out of Kirsty's pocket.

"This is terrible,"

Rachel said. "Those eggs are going bad because the magic egg is missing. We have to find it so Mr. Hopper has some eggs to sell!"

"That's exactly what I was thinking," Kirsty said. "Maybe we can find it at Daffodil Field."

Emma fluttered between the girls.

"I didn't get that magical shiver in the market. It's very strange."

"I'm sure we'll figure it out," Rachel assured her. With that, the girls continued their walk to Daffodil Field. As they got closer, they could hear the sound of the excited crowd. Parents and kids waited along the edge of the field for the event to start. The children clutched colorful Easter baskets.

Rachel gasped at the sight. Hundreds of daffodils bloomed in the grass! The yellow flowers were so bright they looked like the shining sun. The field was so big that Rachel couldn't even see where it ended.

"It's so pretty!" she cried.

"I'll have to paint a picture of this when I get home," Emma said, peeking out of Kirsty's pocket. "Everyone in Fairyland would love to see it!"

Kirsty's dad started talking through a megaphone.

"The Easter egg hunt will begin when the whistle blows!" Mr. Tate announced. "Please don't step on the daffodils as you search. There are plenty of eggs for everyone!"

"Oh, dear," Emma said, suddenly looking nervous. "There are so many kids here. What if one of them finds a magic egg before we do?"

"Don't worry," Rachel said. "I can run really fast."

"Me, too," Kirsty added. "Besides, we know what we're looking for. I'm sure we'll spot one of the magic eggs, if it's here."

The girls walked to the starting line and each grabbed a basket.

Tweeeeet! Mr. Tate blew his whistle.

"Let the Easter egg hunt begin!" he cried.

Daffodil
Disguise

Rachel and Kirsty raced between the rows of daffodils. They spotted many eggs as they ran. Strangely, the eggs weren't bright colors—yellow, green, blue, purple, pink, or orange. The colors were faded, and some were even brown or gray.

"Yuck!" Rachel exclaimed, stopping to look at an egg.

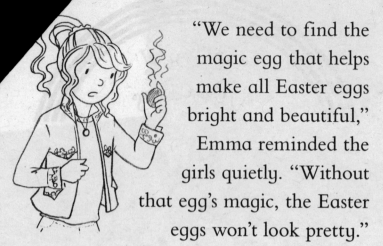

"We need to find the magic egg that helps make all Easter eggs bright and beautiful," Emma reminded the girls quietly. "Without that egg's magic, the Easter eggs won't look pretty."

Kirsty stopped and scanned the field of daffodils. "We're looking for an egg that's white, with a picture painted on it," she said. "That should stick out in this yellow and green field."

Rachel pointed to an area up ahead. "Maybe it's by those big daffodils over there," she suggested.

The girls hurried toward the big daffodils, and Emma fluttered along beside them. They were a few rows

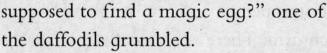

away when Emma suddenly stopped in midair.

"Wait," she warned. "I don't think those are daffodils. Look!"

The daffodils were moving! Not only that, they were talking, too!

"There are so many eggs here! How are we supposed to find a magic egg?" one of the daffodils grumbled.

"Just keep looking," another daffodil said crossly. "Jack Frost will be angry if we don't find one."

"They're goblins!" Rachel realized.

"We'd better duck," Kirsty whispered, crouching down.

The girls got a closer look at the

goblins in disguise. Each goblin wore a hat on his head that looked like a yellow daffodil. His green body and clothes looked like a flower stem. And he had a fake green leaf strapped to each arm. There were at least seven goblins dressed as daffodils!

The goblins started to get loud and rowdy as they searched for the egg.

"It's over there!" one yelled. "No, it's over there!" another one shouted. The goblins tripped over each other as they scrambled to find the magic egg. "*Ow!* You're stepping on my petals!" a goblin whined. "We'd better get moving," Rachel said. "We can't let those goblins beat us to the egg this time!" The girls started looking through the daffodils once more. They hadn't gotten

far when they heard the sound of a child crying.

"Oh, no!" Emma cried. "Someone is in trouble."

A Stinky Problem

The girls hurried toward the sound of the crying child. They found two little girls and a boy standing around a pile of broken eggs. Luckily, there were no goblins around. But something still wasn't right.

Rachel wrinkled her nose. "Those eggs are smelly!"

Kirsty nodded. "They look rotten."

One of the little girls was crying. "These Easter eggs aren't nice. I want my mommy!"

Rachel and Kirsty heard the sound of the goblins getting closer.

"Something smells nice and stinky!" one of the goblins said.

"Just like Mom's cooking! Yum!" agreed another goblin.

Emma peeked out from her hiding place inside Kirsty's pocket. "We have to get these kids away, quickly!" she warned. "Otherwise, they might see the goblins."

Kirsty thought fast and turned back to the children. "We saw some pretty eggs

over there," she said, pointing far away
from the goblins.

The sad little girl wiped the tears from
her cheeks. "Really?"

Kirsty nodded. "Why don't you go
look for them?"

The kids brightened and scampered
away quickly.

Rachel frowned. "Kirsty, that was
a lie!"

"I know," Kirsty replied. "I don't like lying. But we had to get them away from the goblins, and that was the only thing I could think of to do."

"Well, now we have to find the magic egg *fast*!" Rachel said. "If we don't, the whole Easter egg hunt will be ruined."

Emma flew out of Kirsty's pocket. "I'll have a better view if I fly over the field," she said.

"But then everyone might see you," Kirsty reminded her.

Emma thought for a moment, then grinned. "I have an idea."

She waved her wand in a circle. Rainbow-colored sparkles appeared like tiny fireworks in the air.

Then she called out in a singsong voice:

"Help me please, my butterfly friends.
The goblins are up to their evil ends."

Rachel and Kirsty watched, amazed, as the air filled with beautiful butterflies! Their wings shimmered in the sunlight. Some were blue, some were yellow, and some were orange.

Emma laughed and flew up into the middle of the crowd of butterflies. She flapped her delicate wings. "See? If anyone spots me, they'll think I'm a butterfly!"

"Great idea!" Rachel said. "We'll keep looking down here while you search from the sky."

Emma and the butterflies flew off

across the field.

"Finally, that pesky fairy is gone!" a voice cried out.

The girls froze. The daffodils around them jumped up. But they weren't daffodils at all. Rachel and Kirsty were surrounded by goblins!

"Ha! Our plan worked!" a goblin cried, gesturing to his friends. "We'll stay and keep these girls out of the way.

The other goblins will follow that fairy
to the magic egg!"

The group of goblins laughed.

Rachel and Kirsty were a little bit
afraid—but just a little bit. They had
outsmarted Jack Frost's goblins before.

"What should we do?" Kirsty
whispered to Rachel.

"Run past them?" Rachel suggested.

"Maybe, but there are a lot of them,"

Kirsty replied. "They might catch us."

"Hey! No talking!" a goblin snapped.

Kirsty smiled sweetly. "Sorry. We were just saying how pretty you all look!"

The goblins frowned.

"Pretty? We're not pretty! We're goblins!" one of them protested.

"But you look like pretty flowers," Kirsty said.

The goblins grumbled. Rachel smiled at Kirsty. She knew what her friend was trying to do.

"Well, not *all* of you are pretty,"
Rachel said. She pointed to one of the
goblins. "You look scary. In fact, *you*
might be the scariest one."

The goblin looked proud. "Of course!
I'm the scariest of all!"

The other goblins didn't like that.

"No, *I'm* the scariest!"

"No, it's me!"

"Nobody is
scarier than I am!"

The goblins
started to argue.

Soon they were shoving and wrestling each other, just like they had done in the market.

Rachel nudged Kirsty. "They're distracted. Let's run!"

Egg-citement!

Rachel and Kirsty ran right past the fighting goblins. The goblins were so busy arguing, they didn't even notice!

"Now we have to find Emma before the other goblins do," Rachel said.

The girls scanned the field. A few rows away, they saw the butterflies hovering over a small daffodil patch.

"Over there!" Kirsty cried.

The girls ran toward the butterflies. They spotted a small group of goblins running from the other direction.

Kirsty tried to run faster. "They're going to beat us there!"

"Maybe we can stop them," Rachel said.

"How?" Kirsty asked.

Rachel quickly bent and scooped up an Easter egg from under a daffodil leaf. It looked gray and smelled bad.

Kirsty did the same. Their baskets were filled with rotten eggs by the time they reached Emma.

Emma turned her head and waved when she saw them. "I found it!" the fairy called out. "One of the magic eggs!"

The girls saw a white egg perched in the center of a daffodil. It had a picture of a colorful Easter egg painted on it and sparkled with fairy magic.

But two of the goblins had already reached Emma.

"I'll take that!" one of them said,

grabbing for the egg.
Rachel nodded at
Kirsty. "Now!"
The girls pelted
the two goblins with
rotten eggs. The eggs
broke as they hit the goblins, splattering
them with smelly goo.

"Oh, no!" one of them yelled.

"Yuck!" shouted the other. "It's slimy

and cold. This is even worse than having chilly, wet feet!"

They ran off, leaving the magic egg inside the flower.

Kirsty hurried to the daffodil and picked up the egg. Emma fluttered down next to her, smiling widely.

"Good work, girls!" she cheered. "You did a great job getting rid of those goblins." Emma turned to the butterflies. "Thank you for your help!"

The butterflies flew away across the field in a blur of beautiful colors.

Kirsty looked down at the egg in her hand. "This is the magic egg that makes Easter eggs bright and

beautiful, isn't it?"
Emma nodded.
"Yes! I should get it
back to Fairyland
quickly, before any
more goblins show up
to cause trouble."

The fairy waved her wand over the
magic egg. The egg shrank down to its
fairy-size. Then it floated up and landed
in Emma's palm.

"I'll be back soon," Emma told the
girls. "We still have one more magic egg
to find."

"And the Easter
Bunny, too," Rachel
added.

Emma nodded,
blowing each girl a kiss.

She flapped her wings, and the air
around her sparkled and shimmered.
Then she vanished.

Rainbow Magic

Just then, the three little kids they'd seen earlier came running back to Rachel and Kirsty. They looked angry.

"There you are," said the little girl who had been crying. "You told us there were nice eggs over there. But we didn't find any! Just these!"

She held out her Easter basket. It was filled with gray and brown eggs.

"They're all yucky!" complained the little boy next to her. He crossed his arms in front of him.

At that moment, a beautiful rainbow appeared over the field. Everyone began to *ooh* and *ahh* as they peered up at the sky. The rainbow colors sparkled over the whole field of daffodils.

Rachel and Kirsty looked at each other.

"Do you think it's fairy magic?"
Rachel whispered.

"I think so," Kirsty said, gazing
around the field. "Look!"

The gray and brown eggs in the
field were changing color right before
their eyes! Now they were bright pink,
yellow, and blue, with colorful polka
dots and swirly designs.

"Your eggs look very nice to me,"

Kirsty told the little girl.

The three kids looked inside the Easter basket and gasped.

"They're so pretty!" the girl cried.

The little boy's eyes were wide when he looked back up at Kirsty. "You must be magic!"

Kirsty grinned. "It's the magic of Easter," she said. "There are pretty eggs all over the field now," Rachel told them. "You should go find more."

"Hooray!" the kids cheered, running off happily.

"We should get some eggs, too," Kirsty said, turning back to Rachel. "Our parents will wonder why we don't have any if we come back empty-handed."

Rachel looked worried. "I hope there are some left for us!"

The girls raced through the field once again. Now that they didn't have to worry about goblins, it was fun looking for the Easter eggs.

Rachel found a purple one with yellow stars tucked under a daffodil. Kirsty found an orange egg with blue flowers all over it. Each egg they found was nicer than the last.

"Emma's Easter magic is amazing!" Rachel said. "These are the most

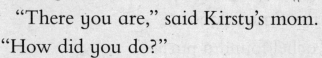

beautiful eggs I've ever seen."

"Me, too!" Kirsty agreed.

When there were no
more eggs on the field,
the girls met up with
their parents at the
starting line.

"There you are," said Kirsty's mom.
"How did you do?"

Kirsty held up her basket. "We found
lots of nice ones!"

Rachel's mom joined them. "Are you
sure?" she asked. "Some of the kids were

complaining that their eggs were rotten."

Mrs. Tate looked around. "That's funny. All of the eggs look fine to me."

Rachel and Kirsty smiled at each other. The magic egg was doing its work! All of the Easter eggs were bright and beautiful again.

"What do you say we head home for some lunch?" Mrs. Tate asked. "I'll make egg salad."

"Yum!" the girls said at the same time.

They rode home in the back of the Tates' car, past the stores in Wetherbury. Through the market window, Rachel and Kirsty could see Mr. Hopper selling a carton of eggs to a

customer. The store owner had a happy
smile on his face.

"Looks like
Mr. Hopper's
shipment of
eggs came
in," Kirsty
remarked.

"Just in
time!"
Rachel
added.

Then
they passed
the pet
shop. The sign on the door read
OPEN.

"I thought the pet shop was closed for
vacation," Kirsty said.

"I thought so, too," said Mrs. Tate from the front seat. "Mrs. Gilligan went to stay with her daughter, who lives by the beach. Maybe she got somebody to watch the store for her."

That seemed a little strange to Kirsty. She thought about it for the rest of the car ride. She brought it up when she and Rachel were eating their

egg salad sandwiches at the picnic table outside.

"I've been thinking about the pet shop," Kirsty began.

Rachel nodded her head eagerly. "Me, too!" she said. "Emma got that magical feeling every time we passed it."

"And it's strange that it was closed for Easter vacation, but now it's open," Kirsty added.

"Strange or *magical*?" Rachel asked, taking a bite of her sandwich.

"Good question," Kirsty said thoughtfully.

"We should go back to the pet shop after lunch," Rachel suggested.

"That's a good idea," Kirsty agreed. "But I think my parents have more Easter plans for us."

"We have to find a way," Rachel said, lowering her voice. "If we don't track down the last missing egg and the Easter Bunny, everyone's Easter plans will be ruined!"

The Easter Bunny Incident

Contents

A Trap

"Mom, what are we doing this afternoon?" Kirsty asked after lunch.

Mrs. Tate smiled. "Mr. and Mrs. Harrison are inviting people to visit Strawberry Farm today," she said. "There were lots of animals born this spring, and we'll get to meet them."

"Oh, baby animals are so cute!"

Rachel exclaimed, grinning. "Will there be lambs?"

Kirsty's mom nodded. "And goats, and calves, and baby ducks, too."

Going to the farm sounded like a lot of fun. But Kirsty and Rachel were worried. They had to find the last missing magic egg *and* the Easter Bunny by the end of the day. If they didn't, Easter wouldn't be the same!

"Do Rachel and I have time to take a walk first?" Kirsty asked.

Mrs. Tate looked at the kitchen clock. "We're leaving for the farm at two o'clock, so you have a little bit of time. Go out and enjoy the beautiful day!"

Kirsty nodded to Rachel, and the girls stepped outside into the bright sunshine.

"Now we'll have time to check out the pet shop," Kirsty said.

"I have a good feeling that we'll find something important there," Rachel added. "There must be a reason why Emma got a magical feeling every time we walked past that place."

Kirsty looked around. "Emma? Are you here?"

The Easter Fairy appeared in a sparkly spray of fairy dust. "King Oberon and

Queen Titania were so happy that we found the second magic egg!" she cried, twirling through the air. "They told me to thank you both."

"We're glad to help," Kirsty said, smiling at her fairy friend. "And we have an idea. We're going back to the pet shop in town. We think something strange is happening there."

"I'll come with you," Emma told them, suddenly looking serious.

Emma flew into Kirsty's pocket and

the friends hurried to the pet shop together. As they turned the corner onto High Street, Emma suddenly spoke up.

"Look! Up there! It's an egg!"

Emma pointed to a crook in the branch of a tree right next to the pet shop. The girls could see something sparkly and white there.

Emma was quivering with excitement. "I'll fly up and get it!"

She darted out of Kirsty's pocket, heading

straight for the egg. But before she reached it, Emma stopped in midair.

"Oh, no!" she cried.

"Emma, what's wrong?" Kirsty asked.

"I'm stuck!" the little fairy said in dismay. "It's Goblin Gossamer! Their pet spiders weave it. It's very, very sticky. I can't move my wings!"

Rachel shaded her eyes with her hand so she could see better. She spotted Emma up above, struggling, but she couldn't see anything else around the fairy. "I don't see a thing," she said, squinting.

"Goblin Gossamer is invisible," Emma told them. "Goblins like to use it to trap fairies. The only way to get out is to sprinkle it with fairy dust."

"Can you use your wand?" Kirsty asked, worried.

"No!" Emma called down. "I can't move my arms."

Rachel's eyes got wide. How could they possibly help Emma now? Then she looked at the locket hanging around Kirsty's neck. Rachel had a matching one of her own. They were presents from the king and queen of the fairies . . . and they were filled with magical fairy dust!

"It's a good thing we have some fairy dust," Rachel said.

She opened up her locket and sprinkled some of the fairy dust onto her palm. Kirsty did the same. Then the two girls blew gently on the fairy dust. It floated into the air, leaving a trail of sparkles behind it.

When the fairy dust swirled around Emma, the invisible Goblin Gossamer became visible. It looked like a green spider web. After a moment, the strands of the web dissolved, and Emma was free!

"Oh, thank you," Emma cried in relief, flying down to the girls. "I could have been trapped there for a long time, if it wasn't for you!"

"The goblins must have set that trap," Rachel guessed. "They were trying to keep you from getting the magic egg back!"

Emma shook her head. "No, that wasn't a magic egg at all. It was a plastic egg sprinkled with glitter."

"Then why set a trap?"

Rachel wondered. She scratched her head. Kirsty frowned. "I think they're trying to keep us away from the pet shop."

Just then, the big town clock began to chime. It was two o'clock!

"Oh, no!" Kirsty cried. "We have to get home fast. We're late!"

Soooo Cute!

Kirsty and Rachel ran back to Kirsty's house as quickly as they could.

"Meet us at Strawberry Farm," Kirsty told Emma as they got close.

Emma flew out of Kirsty's pocket. "See you later!" she called, then vanished in a twinkle of light.

Mrs. Tate and Mrs. Walker were

waiting for the girls in the driveway.

"There you are," Kirsty's mom said, opening the car door. "Your dads are going to stay home and start getting supper ready. We'll take you to the farm."

Kirsty and Rachel climbed into the backseat of the Tates' car.

"I can't wait to see the baby animals," Rachel said eagerly. "We don't have any farms like that in Tippington."

"But your town has lots of other fun

things to do," Kirsty pointed out. "I loved picnicking at Windy Lake."

When they arrived at the farm, the gravel parking lot was filled with cars. The porch of the big white farmhouse was decorated with dangling paper Easter eggs. Next to the house stood a red barn and a grain silo. Visitors were walking around a fenced-in field next to the barn. The air smelled of sweet, fresh hay.

Rachel bolted out of the car and ran to see the baby animals.

"Hey, wait up!" Kirsty called out.

Rachel paused at the fence. "Aw, they're *soooo* cute!"

In the pen in front of her were three small lambs with curly

white wool. Next to them
were two brown-and-white
calves with big, brown eyes.

Gray baby goats munched
on hay in another pen. And in
the last pen, fuzzy
yellow baby ducks
splashed in a small pond.

"They *are* awfully cute," Kirsty agreed.

Rachel reached through the fence to pet one of the lambs. "Hi there, little guy," she said.

Cock-a-doodle-doo!

The loud crow of a rooster rang across the farm.

Rachel jumped. "What was that?" she asked.

"It's a rooster," Kirsty replied.

"Do they have chickens here?" Rachel asked, looking around.

Kirsty nodded. "There's a big coop behind the barn."

Rachel looked thoughtful. After a moment, her eyes lit up. "Kirsty! Where there are chickens . . ."

". . . there are eggs!" Kirsty said, finishing her thought.

The girls looked at each other meaningfully.

"Do you think the last missing magic egg could be in the chicken coop?" Rachel whispered.

Kirsty grinned, her eyes shining. "I think it's a good place to look!"

Together, they walked around the big red barn. Through the open door, they

saw some big cows and sheep munching
on hay.

"Those must be the mommy and
daddy animals," Rachel said.

Kirsty looked around. "I wonder where
Emma is."

They turned the corner of the barn,
and found themselves face-to-face with
a small group of lambs.

"What are you doing out of your pen?" Rachel asked. "Are you lost?"

"No," replied one of the lambs. "But we want *you* to get lost!"

Rachel and Kirsty gasped and stepped back. These weren't baby sheep at all.

They were goblins!

Dancing Chickens

The goblins were wearing fuzzy lamb costumes, but their green heads stuck out from under the fake lamb heads.

Rachel put her hands on her hips. "Get out of our way!" she said bravely.

But the goblins stood in a straight line in front of them, blocking their path.

"No way!" one of the goblins said.

"We're under strict orders from Jack Frost. You girls keep messing everything up!"

"*You're* the ones messing everything up!" Kirsty shot back. "Why can't you just go away and let everyone have a nice Easter?"

The goblins didn't answer. Instead, their eyes grew wide. They looked afraid.

Kirsty and Rachel turned to see Emma flying toward them! Glittering fairy dust drizzled from her wand. All the big cows and sheep were following the fairy dust! When they saw the disguised goblins, their eyes got angry.

"*Moo!*" bellowed the cows.

"*Baaaa!*" cried the sheep.

The animals charged past Kirsty and Rachel and stomped toward the goblins.

"Run!" one of the goblins cried.

The goblins scrambled in all directions, leaving their lamb costumes behind.

Emma flew up to the cows and sheep. "Thank you, my friends," she said kindly.

"*Mooo,*" replied one of the cows, nodding.

The animals slowly returned to the barn, while Emma fluttered over to Rachel and Kirsty.

"You showed up just in time!" Kirsty said gratefully.

"Yes," Rachel added, nodding. "Thank you!"

"Those goblins are such a pain!" Emma replied, frowning. "I hope we've gotten rid of them for a while."

"Me, too," said Kirsty. They had

important things to do! "Rachel and I were just going to the chicken coop to look for the missing egg."

Emma fluttered her wings happily. "Oh, what a wonderful idea! Let's go!"

The chicken coop was a large wooden building with wide shelves built along one side. The shelves held rows of small nesting boxes filled with hay, so the chickens could lay their eggs there. Almost every box had a fat, white chicken sitting on it.

"Where are the eggs?" Rachel asked, looking around.

"Underneath the chickens," Kirsty explained. "They sit on the eggs after they lay them. I've helped Mr. and Mrs. Harrison collect the eggs before. But the chickens don't always like it. Sometimes they put up a fuss."

"Then it won't be easy to look for the magic egg, will it?" Rachel asked.

"I know a way," Emma said brightly. "Back home, my pet chicken, Fluffy, loves to dance. This is her favorite song."

Emma began to sing in her musical fairy voice.

"Cluck, cluck, cluck! Cluck, cluck, cluck!"
Emma's voice carried through the

coop. The happy chickens stood up one by one, hopping from one foot to the other. "That's amazing!" Rachel said, her eyes wide in wonder.

Kirsty ran to the nesting boxes and

looked under one of the chickens. "If
there's a magic egg here, we'll find it."

"Wonderful!" Emma exclaimed. "You
girls can sing along with me, too, if you
want."

"*Cluck, cluck, cluck! Cluck, cluck, cluck!*"
Rachel and Kirsty joined in. Now all
of the chickens were standing up. Some
moved their heads back and forth to
the music.

The girls raced along the rows of
boxes, hoping to spot the magic egg. At

first, they saw one plain white egg after another. But then they both noticed something at the same time.

The biggest chicken in the coop was standing over a beautiful, sparkly egg! As the girls got closer, they could see that it had a picture of an Easter basket painted on it.

Kirsty gingerly reached underneath the chicken and grabbed the egg. It glittered with fairy magic in her hand.

"We did it!" Kirsty cried. "We found the last magic egg!"

A Pet Shop Surprise

"Oh, this is amazing!" Emma cried happily. She flew to Kirsty and waved her wand over the magic egg. It shrunk down to fairy-size, and Emma scooped it up. "Once I return this to Fairyland, the Easter Bunny will have the magic he needs to deliver baskets to boys and girls everywhere."

Kirsty frowned. "But we still have to find the Easter Bunny," she reminded the little fairy.

Emma nodded. "I know. But I'm very hopeful. Thanks to you girls, we've found the three magic eggs. Somehow, I just know we'll find the Easter Bunny."

"We'll do our best," Rachel said.

"I need to bring this egg to Fairyland," Emma told them. "But I'll come back and find you as soon as I can."

"And we'll keep looking for the Easter Bunny," Kirsty promised.

Emma waved to them as she vanished in a swirl of twinkling light. By now, the chickens were all sitting on their nests again.

"We should try to go back to the pet store," Kirsty suggested. "I just have a feeling about that place."

"Right," Rachel agreed. "Only this time, we need to keep an eye out for goblin traps!"

The girls walked back to the pens where the baby animals were kept. Mrs. Walker and Mrs. Tate were feeding corn to the baby goats.

"That tickles!" Rachel's mom said with a laugh. She looked up when she saw the girls. "Are you having fun?"

"Definitely!" Rachel said. "Mom, can we get a baby lamb at our house?"

"I don't think we have room in our backyard," Mrs. Walker replied.

"But you can always visit us and come back to Strawberry Farm whenever you like," Mrs. Tate said.

Mrs. Walker brushed the corn crumbs off of her hands. "We should wash up before we head home."

"I need to stop at the market on the way back," said Mrs. Tate.

That gave Kirsty an idea. "Can I show Rachel the pet shop while you're shopping?"

"I don't see why not," her mom

replied. "It's just a few doors down."

Kirsty and Rachel looked at each other. They were both thinking the same thing: Maybe they would finally find out what was happening in the pet shop!

When they got to town, Kirsty and Rachel waved to their moms and cautiously walked up to the pet shop. They saw a sparkly white egg sitting on top of a mailbox nearby.

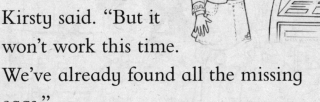

"Another trap!" Kirsty said. "But it won't work this time. We've already found all the missing eggs."

A bell tinkled as they pushed open the door of the pet shop. Half of the store was filled with shelves stocked with pet food, toys, and bowls. The other half was filled with tanks and cages of small pets — lizards, snakes, hamsters, and rabbits. A few customers were looking at the animals, while others shopped for different supplies.

Kirsty and Rachel walked through the aisles, looking around.

"Everything seems normal," Rachel

remarked. She shrugged.

"I know," Kirsty said. "I wish Emma were here. She could tell us if she felt something magical."

Suddenly, Rachel stopped. "Kirsty, look over there!"

Rachel pointed to the big pen in the corner set up for rabbits. It held a small, brown rabbit, a black-and-white rabbit with floppy ears, and a fluffy, white

rabbit. The white rabbit was sparkling with fairy magic!

"Do you think it could be the Easter Bunny?" Kirsty whispered.

"May I help you, girls?" asked a voice behind them.

The girls spun around and gasped. They knew that voice!

"Jack Frost! What are you doing here?" Rachel asked bravely.

Jack Frost grinned. He was taller than the goblins, with spiky white hair, and a pointy nose and ears.

"I'm sorry, my name is Mr. Jackson," he said. "I'm a friend of Mrs. Gilligan's. She asked me to watch the shop while she's away."

"You can't fool us!" Kirsty said, crossing her arms. "We know what you're doing. You've kidnapped the Easter Bunny!"

Jack Frost chuckled coldly. "What lively imaginations you have. Now, if you don't mind, I must ask you to leave the store. You're disturbing the customers."

"But we're not—" Rachel began, but Kirsty stopped her.

"Come on, Rachel," she said.

Rachel and Kirsty left the shop.

"Why did we leave?" Rachel asked, confused. "I think that white bunny in the pen might be the Easter Bunny!"

"I do, too," Kirsty said. "But Jack Frost isn't like an ordinary goblin. He's got powerful magic. We can't beat him without Emma's help!"

Happy Easter!

"Here I am!" Emma cried just then, popping into the air in front of them. "The last magic egg is safe in Fairyland."

"Jack Frost is inside the pet shop!" Kirsty told her immediately.

"And we think we found the Easter Bunny," Rachel added. "But we're not sure. It looks like a regular white rabbit, but it's all sparkly, like it might be magical."

Emma clapped her hands together. "Oh, that's fabulous news! Jack Frost must be using a spell to make the Easter Bunny look like an ordinary rabbit. That's not his true form, of course. We must get him

back right away!"

"But Jack Frost is guarding the shop," Kirsty pointed out. "How will we get past him?"

Emma was thoughtful. "We need a distraction of some kind. Then I can fly in, wave my wand over the

Easter Bunny, and send him home."

Just then, a group of grumbling goblins approached on the empty sidewalk. The goblins looked dirty, and some of them had fake wool from their lamb costumes stuck to their green skin.

"Jack Frost is going to be so mad!" said one goblin.

"We didn't find the magic egg!" wailed another.

"It wasn't our fault! It was those terrifying cows and sheep," complained another.

Emma grinned. "Goblins always make a good distraction!" she said brightly. Then she whispered her idea to the girls. "Do you think you can do it?"

Kirsty nodded. "Just watch." She turned to Rachel. "I'm so excited!" she said in a loud voice.

"Me, too!" shouted Rachel. "The last

magic egg is inside the pet shop."
"But it's in the snake tank," Kirsty
replied loudly, biting her lip. "I'm
too scared to reach into the
tank to get it!"
The goblins
raced up
to them.
"We're
not scared!"
one of them
bragged.
"We're going
to get that magic
egg before you do!"
taunted another.
The goblins ran into the pet
shop, with the girls and Emma close
behind. They peeked around a shelf and

watched as the goblins pulled open the lid of the snake tank. Then they started picking up the snakes and waving them in the air.

"Where is it? Where is the magic egg?" they cried.

The snakes slid out of their hands and started crawling on the floor.

Jack Frost came around the corner — and he was furious. "What are you doing?" he screamed at his goblins. "Put those snakes down!"

Emma winked at Rachel and Kirsty, and flew to the rabbit pen. Jack Frost was so busy yelling that he didn't even see her.

The girls watched as Emma waved her magic wand over the Easter Bunny three times. A cloud of glittering fairy

dust surrounded the rabbit. The cloud
lifted the white bunny up, up, up, into
the air.

That's when Jack Frost finally noticed.
"No!" he yelled. He ran toward the
rabbit pen.

But he was too late.

Poof! The Easter Bunny disappeared.

"That's not fair!" Jack Frost cried,

swatting at Emma. But she only giggled before vanishing, too. "Jack Frost looks really angry," Rachel remarked. "We'd better get out of here," Kirsty whispered, edging quietly toward the door.

The girls ran back to the market as quickly as they could.

Back home, Rachel and Kirsty helped get dinner ready. Afterward, they played board games with their parents. There was no sign of Emma anywhere!

They couldn't talk about what had happened that day until bedtime, since their parents might hear. Kirsty snuggled

into her bed, and Rachel pulled up the covers on hers.

"I wonder where Emma is," Kirsty said.

"It's the night before Easter," Rachel reminded her. "I'm sure she's very busy."

Kirsty yawned. "I guess so. I just hope she got back to Fairyland okay."

"I know she did," Rachel said. "We saw her. And all three magic eggs are back, too."

"That's right," Kirsty agreed. "That means that Easter candy will taste delicious, Easter eggs will be bright and beautiful, and the Easter Bunny will deliver baskets to boys and girls all over the world."

Kirsty's door opened, and Kirsty's mom peeked inside.

"Go to sleep, girls," she said. "The Easter Bunny is coming tonight!"

"We know, Mom," Kirsty said, winking at Rachel.

The girls drifted off into a deep sleep. In the morning, they both woke up at the same time. Bright sunlight shone through the window. Outside, the spring birds were singing a happy song.

"The Easter Bunny!" Kirsty and Rachel cried.

They scrambled out of bed and ran downstairs. On the kitchen table were two beautiful Easter baskets. A tag on one read KIRSTY, and the other read RACHEL.

"He came!" Rachel said.

The girls' parents came into the kitchen, yawning.

"I see the Easter Bunny visited last night," Rachel's dad said with a grin.

Kirsty grabbed her basket. "Come on!" she told Rachel. "Let's see what he brought."

The girls took their baskets onto the sunny porch and sat on the steps. They looked through the shiny Easter grass.

Kirsty found a chocolate egg and popped it into her mouth. "Yum!"

Rachel ate a blue jellybean. "It tastes like blueberries!"

"And look," Kirsty said, picking up a dyed Easter egg with purple and pink swirls. "It's bright and beautiful!"

Then Kirsty saw the grass in her Easter basket start to move. Out flew the best Easter surprise of all — Emma!

"Happy Easter!" she cried, hovering in front of the girls.

"Happy Easter, Emma!" the girls said together, grinning.

"King Oberon and Queen Titania are so happy that you helped us find the Easter Bunny," Emma said. "They sent you each a special gift. Go ahead, look inside your baskets."

The girls eagerly dug through the brightly colored Easter grass. At the same time, they each pulled out a beautiful golden egg.

"Open them up!" Emma told them.

Each egg had a hinge on the back, and they opened right in the middle. A beautiful tune began to play, and inside, a tiny fairy in a yellow dress twirled around and around.

"Emma, that's you!" Kirsty realized.

Emma clapped her hands, delighted. "Aren't they wonderful?"

"She looks just like you," Rachel said. "Please make sure to thank the king and queen for us."

"Of course!" Emma said. She twirled around in the air in front of them. "Well, I have to head off now. Today is a busy day! But thanks again, girls. Have a happy Easter!"

Rachel and Kirsty smiled at each other. "We definitely will!"